Two Brothers

Weekly Reader Children's Book Club presents

Two Brothers

by Eugene Schwarz

Translated from the Russian
by Elizabeth Reynolds Hapgood

Pictures by Gabriel Lisowski

HARPER & ROW, PUBLISHERS
New York, Evanston, San Francisco, London

TWO BROTHERS

English-language translation copyright © 1973
by Elizabeth Reynolds Hapgood

Illustrations copyright © 1973 by Gabriel Lisowski

Library of Congress Catalog Card Number: 72-9868
Trade Standard Book Number: 06-025248-0
Harpercrest Standard Book Number: 06-025249-9

Weekly Reader Children's Book Club Edition

This book is dedicated to all who believe in kindness. Kindness melts the ice. Eugene Schwarz believed that. I hope you do.

Elizabeth Reynolds Hapgood
New York City
November, 1972

Trees do not know how to talk. They stand still, rooted to one spot. Yet they are alive, they breathe, they grow all their lives. Even huge, ancient trees grow every year. And just as shepherds care for their flocks, so do the foresters look after their woods.

Now, once upon a time a forester lived in a great forest and his name was Blackbeard. All day he walked back and forth through the forest, and in his own district he knew every single tree by name.

While he was among his trees the forester was happy, but when he was at home he often sighed and looked sad. Everything was peaceful in the forest, but at home he was troubled by his two sons, Big Brother and Little Brother. The older boy was twelve and the younger boy was seven. No matter how hard the forester reasoned with his two sons, no matter how much he begged them—the brothers quarrelled every day.

One morning, it was the twenty-eighth of December, the forester told his two sons that they would not have a New Year's celebration that year. If they were to have a party both he and his wife would have to go to town to get decorations. Their mother couldn't go alone because the wolves would eat her. He couldn't go alone because he did not know what to buy. And they could not go together and leave the boys alone, because Big Brother would mistreat Little Brother.

Big Brother was clever. He did well in school, read a great deal, and could be very persuasive. He convinced his father that he would not mistreat his brother and that everything in the house would be kept in order until their parents returned from town.

"Will you promise this?" asked Father.

"I give you my word of honor," answered Big Brother.

"Very well then," said Father. "We shall be gone three days. We will be back at eight o'clock on the evening of the thirty-first. Until then you will be the master here. You will be responsible for the house, but especially for your brother. You will be a father to him. See to it!"

Their mother prepared food for three dinners, three lunches, and three breakfasts, and showed the boys

how to heat them up. Their father brought in firewood for three days and gave Big Brother a box of
matches. Then he harnessed the horse to the sleigh.
The sleigh bells tinkled, the runners crunched the
snow, and the parents rode off.

Everything went well the first day. The second
day, even better.

Then the thirty-first of December arrived. At six
o'clock Big Brother gave Little Brother his supper
and then sat down to read *Sinbad the Sailor*. He had
just reached the most interesting part and was anxious to know what happened next when Little
Brother interrupted. "I am lonely, please play with
me," he said.

Big Brother became angry. "Leave me alone!" he
yelled. That was the way all their quarrels started.
Big Brother ignored the interruptions as long as he
could. Then he grabbed Little Brother by the scruff
of his neck. "Leave me alone," he yelled and pushed
Little Brother out into the yard and closed the door.

It was pitch black outside. Little Brother was
frightened. He banged on the door and screamed,
"What are you doing to me? My father would never
do this to me!"

Big Brother took one step in the direction of the
door but then he said to himself, "All right, I'll read

five lines and then I'll let him in. Nothing can happen to him in that time."

So Big Brother settled himself into an armchair and buried his nose in his book. When he finally looked up, the clock hands pointed to a quarter to eight. Big Brother jumped up. "What have I done!" he cried. "Little Brother is out in the cold alone— and without a coat!"

He rushed out into the yard. It was pitch black and there was not a sound anywhere. Big Brother called his brother at the top of his voice, but no one replied. Then he lighted a lantern and looked in every corner of the yard.

Fresh snow lay on the ground, but there was not a footprint to be seen. Little Brother had vanished. Big Brother began to cry bitterly and to beg his brother's forgiveness. But nothing did any good. There was no reply.

The clock struck eight, and at that instant Big Brother heard sleigh bells in the distance.

"Mother and Father are returning," he thought sadly. "Oh, if only I could turn the clock back two hours. I wouldn't have locked my brother out. We would be standing here together, happy to have our parents back."

The sleigh bells tinkled louder and louder: now

Big Brother could hear the horse snorting, the runners crunching the snow, and the sleigh coming to a standstill. His father jumped out, his black beard frosted with snow. His mother climbed out of the sleigh with a large basket in her hands. They both looked so happy.

"Why did you come out without your coat?" asked his mother.

"Where's Little Brother?" asked his father.

Big Brother could not say a word.

"Where is your brother?" his father asked again.

Big Brother burst into tears. His father took him by the arm and led him inside. His mother followed them silently. Big Brother told them the whole story and then he looked at his father. It was warm inside the house but the snow on his beard had not melted. His father's beard was *not* white with snow; he was so heartbroken that his hair had turned completely white.

"Put your coat on and go out," said his father quietly. "And do not dare return until you have found your brother."

"What are you doing?" cried his mother. "Must we lose both our children?" His father made no reply.

Big Brother put on his coat, took the lantern, and left the house.

He walked and called, walked and called, but no one answered. The familiar forest enclosed him like a wall but he felt alone. The trees are, of course, living creatures, but they do not know how to talk, and they stand rooted in one spot. Besides, during the winter they sleep soundly. So Big Brother had no one to talk to. He walked past places where he had often raced with his younger brother. Now it was difficult for him to understand why they always quarrelled. He remembered how thin Little Brother was and how some of the hair on top of his head always stood on end; how he laughed when his older brother joked with him; and how happy he was when he was included in his brother's games. Big Brother was so filled with pity for his younger brother that he did not notice the cold, or the dark, or the silence. At times he became frightened, and looked all around him, the way a rabbit does. He was, after all, twelve years old, but next to the huge trees in the forest he felt very small.

After reaching the end of his father's district, he came to that of their neighbor forester who played a game of chess with his father every Sunday. Then Big Brother crossed the district of a forester whom he saw every three months, then one whom he saw once in six months, and another whom he saw only once a year. The candle in his lantern had long since burned out, but he walked on and on, faster and faster.

He passed the districts belonging to foresters about whom he had only heard. Then his path led upward. When dawn broke, Big Brother saw mountains all around him, and they were covered with dense forests.

Big Brother stopped. He knew that it took seven weeks to ride from his home to the mountains. How had he climbed so far in only one night?

Suddenly he heard a sound in the distance. At first he thought it was only a ringing in his ears. He began to tremble with joy when he thought it might be sleigh bells. Perhaps his younger brother had been found and his father was coming to take them both home. Yet the sound came no nearer, and Big Brother had never heard sleigh bells ring so gently or so evenly.

"I'll go and see where the sound comes from," said the boy.

He walked for one hour, for two hours, three hours. The sound grew louder and louder and he found himself surrounded by strange trees—tall pines on all sides—and they were *transparent* like glass. Their crests shone brightly in the sun. The

pines swayed in the wind and their branches struck each other, giving off a ringing sound.

Farther on, he found transparent fir trees, transparent birches, transparent maples. A huge transparent oak stood in a glade and gave off deep sounds like a bumblebee. Then Big Brother slipped and looked down at the ground. The earth in this forest was also transparent! The dark roots of the trees were transparent. Like great serpents they writhed and twined in the earth and crawled away into its depths.

The boy went over to a birch tree and broke off a twig. While he was looking at it, it melted in his hands. Big Brother realized that the whole forest, frozen to its core, was made of ice, that it was growing in icy ground, and that its roots were also made of ice.

"Why am I not cold?" asked Big Brother, surprised.

"Because I ordered so," came the answer in a shrill, resonant voice.

Big Brother looked around. Behind him stood a tall old man in a greatcoat, hat, and boots—all made of pure snow. His beard and mustache were of icicles, and tinkled gently when he spoke. The old man looked intensely at the boy. His face was neither

good nor evil, and so motionless it made Big Brother's heart tighten.

The old man was silent for a while and then he began to speak in distinct, even tones, as though he were reading out of a book.

"I ordered. That the cold. Should not. Cause you. For the time being. The least harm. Do you know who I am?"

"You are Grandfather Frost," answered the boy.

"I certainly am not!" was the old man's cold reply. "Grandfather Frost is my son. I put my curse on him because he's too good-natured. I, *Great*-grandfather Frost, am different, my young friend. Follow me."

The old man led the way, walking noiselessly over the ice in his soft snow-white boots.

Soon they halted before a sheer cliff. Great-grandfather Frost dug into his great snow overcoat and pulled out a huge key made of ice. It clicked in the lock, and great ice portals swung open in the side of the cliff.

"Follow me," repeated the old man.

"But I have to search for my brother!" exclaimed Big Brother.

"Your brother is here," said Great-grandfather Frost quietly. "Follow me."

They entered a palace built into the side of a mountain, and the great portals shut behind them. The boy found himself in an immense hall of ice. Through great doors, left ajar, he could see another hall, and another, and yet another. There seemed to be no end to the huge, empty halls. On the walls were round lighted lanterns made of ice. Over the door to the next hall was an ice tablet with the number "2" on it.

"Here in my palace there are forty-nine rooms like this one. Follow me," ordered Great-grandfather Frost.

The ice floor was so slippery that Big Brother fell twice, but the old man did not even notice. He strode ahead with even steps and halted only when he came to room number "25."

In the middle of the room was a tall, white-tiled stove. The boy was delighted to see it. Suddenly he was anxious to warm himself. But an icy blast came from the stove. There were ice logs burning in it and they gave off black flames, making black reflections on the icy floor. Great-grandfather Frost sat down on an ice bench and stretched his icy fingers toward the ice flames.

"Sit down beside me," he said to Big Brother. "Let's freeze together."

The boy did not answer.

The old man settled himself comfortably and froze

until the ice logs turned into ice ashes. Then Great-grandfather Frost filled the stove with more ice logs and lighted them with ice matches.

"Now I shall devote a little time to speaking with you," he said to the boy. "You. Must. Listen. To me. Carefully. Understand?"

Big Brother nodded.

Great-grandfather Frost continued to speak in the same distinct way.

"You drove. Your younger brother. Out into the cold. So that. He would. Leave you alone. You like. To be alone. As I do. You. Will. Stay here. Forever. Understand?"

"But they are waiting for us at home," the boy protested.

"You. Will. Stay here. Forever," repeated Great-grandfather Frost.

He went over to the stove and shook the skirts of his great snow overcoat. Out fell all kinds of birds: titmice, nuthatches, woodpeckers, and small forest animals. A pile of them lay on the floor, disheveled and numb. Big Brother winced.

"These bothersome creatures wouldn't leave the forest in peace even in winter," said the old man.

"Are they dead?" asked the boy.

"I have stunned them, but they are not quite dead,"

replied Great-grandfather Frost. "Now they must be turned in front of the stove until they become transparent and ice-like. This is your job. Get on. With this. Useful work. Immediately."

"I'll run away!" cried Big Brother.

"You won't do anything of the sort!" said Great-grandfather Frost firmly. "Your brother is locked up in room number '49.' I know you will not go away and leave him. You will soon get used to life here. Start working."

The boy sat down in front of the stove and with trembling fingers picked up a woodpecker. It seemed to him that the little bird was still breathing. Great-grandfather Frost was watching him intently. Slowly Big Brother brought the bird up to the icy flames. Sadly he watched the feathers of the helpless bird turn white as snow. Then its whole body became hard as stone. When it was as transparent as glass, the old man said, "It's ready now. Take the next."

The boy worked late into the night, and Great-grandfather Frost stood motionless beside him. Finally he put all the ice birds into a sack and asked, "Are your hands cold?"

"No," replied Big Brother.

"That is because I have ordered that for the time being the cold may not do you any harm," said the old man. "But remember. If you. Don't. Obey me. Then I shall. Freeze you. Sit here. Wait. I'll be back. Soon."

Great-grandfather Frost took the sack and disappeared into the recesses of the palace. Somewhere far, far away, a door slammed loudly and the sound echoed through the halls. Great-grandfather Frost returned with the empty sack.

"It is time to go to sleep," he said pointing to a bed made of ice, which stood in the corner. The old man lay down on a bed at the other end of the hall and soon Big Brother heard him snoring. After a long while Big Brother dozed off also. It was morning when the old man shook the boy awake.

"Go into the pantry," he said. "The door is in that left-hand corner. Bring breakfast number '1.' It is on shelf number '9.' "

The boy went to the pantry. It was very large—as big as a hall. Frozen food lay on all the shelves. He put breakfast number "1" on an ice platter and carried it back. There was meat, tea, and bread—all frozen. Big Brother had to gnaw or suck the food like icicles. When Great-grandfather had finished eating he said, "I'm going out to work. You may wander through all the rooms and even go out of the palace, if you wish. Good-bye for now, my young apprentice." With that, Great-grandfather Frost slowly strode out in his great white snow boots.

The instant Great-grandfather Frost left, Big Brother rushed to room number "49." He ran, he fell, he called his brother at the top of his lungs, but only an echo answered him. Finally he reached the forty-ninth room. All other doors except the one which read "49" were open. This last door was tightly shut.

"Little Brother!" called Big Brother. "I have come to rescue you. Are you there?"

". . . You there?" answered the echo.

The great frozen door was made from a solid slab of oak. Big Brother clawed at it with his fingers but they only slid over the surface. He couldn't so much as dislodge a chip of ice.

Slowly, sadly, Big Brother walked back to the entrance hall, and almost at once Great-grandfather Frost entered it too.

After they had eaten their icy dinner, the boy worked late into the night turning the hapless birds, squirrels, and rabbits in front of the ice fire.

And so it went, day after day, after day.

Every day Big Brother thought about the same thing: how to break down that ice oak door. He searched the pantry. He pulled out and peered behind all the bags of frozen cabbages, frozen grain, frozen nuts, hoping to find an axe. Finally he did find one, but when he took it to number "49" it grazed off the ice oak door as if from a smooth stone.

Still the boy kept thinking. Awake or asleep, he thought about one and the same thing.

The old man praised him for his obedience. Standing beside the stove, watching Big Brother turn the birds, rabbits, and squirrels into ice, Great-grandfather Frost would say, "No, I did not make a mistake about you, my young friend. 'Leave me alone!' These are great words. With these words people are constantly causing the destruction of their brothers. 'Leave me alone!' These. Are. Great. Words. One. Day. They will establish. Eternal. Quiet. On earth."

Big Brother imagined the whole world turned into endless rooms of ice, and shuddered.

The old man liked to recall the most ancient of times when great glaciers covered most of the earth. "Ah, how quiet and beautiful it was to live then in the great, quiet cold world!" he would say, and as he spoke his icy whiskers tinkled gently. "I was young then and full of strength. Where have my dear friends, the quiet, massive, gigantic mammoths gone? How I loved to talk with them! To be sure, their language was difficult. The huge beasts used words of incredible length. To pronounce even one such word, in the mammoth language, it was necessary to spend two or even three days and nights. But. We. Were. In. No hurry. To go. Anywhere."

Great-grandfather Frost told many stories, but the boy could think only of how to rescue his brother. One night as Great-grandfather Frost was telling one of his stories, Big Brother suddenly began to jump up and down with excitement.

"What does this improper behavior signify?" asked the old man.

Big Brother did not say a word but his heart was thumping with joy. When one keeps thinking about one and the same thing all the time inevitably one finds a solution. The matches! Big Brother remembered that he still had the matches his father had given him before the trip to town.

The next morning, Great-grandfather Frost had scarcely left for his work when the boy took the axe and rope from the pantry and ran out of the palace.

The old man had gone to the left, so Big Brother ran to the right, where the live forest stood. On the very edge of the woods he found an enormous pine lying on the snow. He chopped pieces from it with his axe and ran back to the palace with a load of firewood.

Big Brother laid a large pile of logs on the thresh-

old of number "49." His match flamed, the kindling caught fire, and soon the whole pile was ablaze. Big Brother laughed with joy. He sat beside the fire and warmed himself.

At first the ice oak door glistened and shone so brightly that it hurt his eyes. Then the surface became covered with little drops of water. When the fire died down Big Brother saw that the door had melted slightly.

"Hooray!" he cried and smote the door with the axe, but it grazed off. The surface was still as hard as rock. "Never mind," he said. "Tomorrow I'll begin all over."

That evening, as he was sitting in front of the ice stove, Big Brother took a little tit and hid it inside his sleeve. Great-grandfather Frost did not notice it. The next day, when Big Brother made a bonfire again, he held the little bird out toward the flames.

He waited and waited, and suddenly its little beak began to tremble, its eyes opened, and it looked at him.

"Hello little bird," was all Big Brother said, although he was almost crying with happiness. "You just wait, Great-grandfather Frost! We will *all* come back to life!"

Every day Big Brother warmed birds, squirrels,

and rabbits back to life. He fixed little hiding places for his new friends in the dark corners of the rooms. He bedded them with moss which he brought back from the live forest. It was cold for them at night but every morning they clustered around the bonfire and stored up enough heat for the night.

Big Brother melted bags of cabbages, grain, and nuts, and fed them to his friends as he played with them in front of the fire. Sometimes he told them about Little Brother and it seemed to him that the birds and the squirrels and the rabbits understood what he was saying.

One day when Big Brother made his bonfire, none of his friends came out of their hiding places to join him. Big Brother was on the point of asking, "Where are you?" when a heavy, icy hand pulled him roughly away from the fire.

Great-grandfather Frost had stolen up behind him in his noiseless snow boots. He blew on the fire. The logs turned transparent and the flames became black. When the iced firewood died down, the ice oak door stood there as strong and as solid as it had been so many days before.

"One more time and I will freeze you!" said Great-grandfather Frost. He picked up the axe and hid it in the enormous folds of his great snow coat.

Big Brother wept for a whole day. When night came he was so tired and unhappy he slept like a log. In his sleep he felt someone tapping him on the cheek. He opened his eyes and saw a little rabbit. Then he saw all of his friends gathered around his icy bed. They came out of their hiding places to help him escape now that Great-grandfather Frost was asleep.

Seven squirrels hopped over to the icy bed of Great-grandfather Frost. They hunted around for a long time in the snow of his greatcoat. They burrowed and burrowed. Suddenly there was a tinkle.

"Leave me alone," growled the old man in his sleep.

The squirrels jumped off his bed and ran over to Big Brother. They were carrying a huge ring full of icy keys in their teeth.

Big Brother understood. With the keys in his hand he rushed to number "49," his friends jumping, flying, and hopping after him.

There before him was the great ice oak door.

Big Brother found the key marked "49." But where was the keyhole? He looked for it in vain.

A nuthatch flew up to the door. With his claws he clutched the rough bark surface of the oak, and crawled over it, head downward. He found something. He chirped in a low tone. Seven woodpeckers flew to the spot and patiently hacked away at the ice with their sharp beaks. They pecked and they pecked and they pecked. Suddenly a square plate of ice fell to the floor and smashed to pieces, revealing the keyhole!

Big Brother inserted the key and turned it. The lock made a clicking sound. The door slowly opened with a rasping noise. Full of excitement, the boy entered the room. The floor was littered with piles of transparent ice animals.

On top of a table made of ice stood his Little Brother. He was staring straight ahead, tears glistening on his cheeks. He was completely transparent, his face, his hands, his jacket, the cowlick on top of his head, his tears—all were ice. He did not breathe or speak. Big Brother whispered, "Let us run, I beg of you, let us run! Mama is waiting for us! Let us hurry home!"

Without waiting for an answer he took his younger brother in his arms and cautiously ran through the icy halls to the palace exit. All his animal friends flew, hopped, and jumped after him.

The sun had just risen. The ice trees shone brightly. Big Brother ran cautiously toward the live

forest, afraid he might stumble and drop Little Brother.

Suddenly he heard a great roar behind him. Great-grandfather Frost was shouting "Boy! Boy! Boy!" in such a thundering voice that all the ice trees trembled.

It became very cold. Big Brother felt his feet getting numb with cold and his arms felt powerless.

"Stop!" commanded the old man.

Big Brother stopped. He was numb.

The animals clustered around, warming him. Big Brother came to life and ran on, protecting Little Brother with all his strength.

The old man was catching up, but Big Brother did not dare run faster—the icy ground was slippery. Just when he thought he was losing ground the rabbits began to turn somersaults under the feet of the evil old man, making him fall. As soon as Great-grandfather Frost raised himself the rabbits would play the same trick, felling him over and over and over. They were trembling with fright, but they had to save their friend. When Great-grandfather Frost rose for the last time, Big Brother, still carrying his brother in his arms, was far down the mountain and into the live forest.

Great-grandfather Frost wept with rage. And as

he wept it began to grow warmer. Big Brother saw the snow melting all around him and the streams running down the ravines. Below, in the foothills, the buds on the trees began to burst open.

"Look—a snowdrop!" cried Big Brother joyfully. Little Brother did not say anything. He was still motionless.

"Never mind. Papa knows how to fix everything!" said Big Brother to Little Brother. "He'll bring you back to life. He will *surely* bring you back to life."

Big Brother ran on and on as fast as he could, holding Little Brother in his arms. When he had set out to find his younger brother, he had climbed the mountain quickly, but coming back down he raced like a whirlwind. He was so happy he had found Little Brother! Now he passed the districts that belonged to the foresters he had only heard of and those of the foresters he saw only every six months and those he saw only every three months. The nearer he came to his home the warmer was the air around him. His rabbit friends hopped for joy, his squirrel friends jumped from branch to branch overhead, his bird friends flew around and twittered. The trees do not know how to talk but they rustled for joy—for their leaves were out and it was spring.

Then Big Brother slipped! He fell into a dip in

the ground near an old maple tree. Little Brother struck the roots of the tree and broke into little pieces.

A great quiet fell over the forest. And out of the snow shrilled a familiar voice, "Of course. I did. It. You. Cannot. Get away. From me. So. Easily!"

Big Brother dropped to the ground, weeping bitterly. Nothing could console him. He wept and wept until he fell asleep in his grief.

The birds came and put the pieces of Little Brother together. The squirrels, with their clever paws, glued the bones in place with sap from the birch trees. Then they all cloaked Little Brother with the warmth of their bodies. When the sun rose they went away. Little Brother lay in the radiant sunlight which warmed him. The tears on his face dried up. His eyes closed softly. His hands were warm. The color came back into his striped jacket. His shoes turned black. Even the cowlick lay softly on the crown of his head. Little Brother heaved a sigh, and another, and began to breathe with a regular and quiet rhythm.

When Big Brother woke, there was Little Brother, alive and unharmed, sleeping on a little rise in the ground. Big Brother jumped up, not believing his eyes. The birds twittered, the forest rustled, and the brooks babbled happily in the ravines.

Big Brother rushed over to Little Brother and grabbed him by the arm. Little Brother opened his eyes and said, "Oh, it's you. What time is it?"

Big Brother put his arms around him and helped him up, and they ran toward home.

Their father and mother were sitting in silence by the window. Father's face was as severe and stern as it was on the evening when he ordered Big Brother to go out and find Little Brother.

"How noisy the birds are today," said Mother.

"They are enjoying the warm weather," replied Father.

"The squirrels are tearing around from branch to branch," said Mother.

"They, too, are glad spring has come," answered Father.

"Can you hear something?" cried Mother suddenly.

"No," answered Father. "Why?"

"Someone is running this way!" said Mother.

"No," said Father sadly. "All winter I kept imagining I heard footsteps crunching the snow outside our windows. No one is running in our direction."

But Mother was already out in the yard, crying, "The children! The children!"

Mother and Father ran forward to meet them.

After they all went into the house, Big Brother looked at his father in amazement. His beard, which had been white when Big Brother left, was turning black in front of his eyes.

After this the forester and his family lived happily.

Now and then Big Brother still says to Little Brother, "Leave me alone!" But he immediately goes on to say, "Not for long, just for ten minutes, please."

And Little Brother agrees, because now the two brothers live together in true friendship.

About the Author

EUGENE SCHWARZ was born in Kazan, Russia, in 1896, and died in Leningrad in 1958. He attended the Law School of Moscow University, but was far more interested in the theatre. By 1923 he had published many stories, novels, film scripts, and fairy tales for children. His film *Don Quixote* won critical praise in the United States and his play *The Dragon* has been performed all over the world.

About the Translator

ELIZABETH REYNOLDS HAPGOOD was born in New York City, where she still lives. She received a diploma in Russian Studies from the University of Paris, and was the first woman in the United States named to the faculty of a men's college when she founded the Russian department at Dartmouth. Mrs. Hapgood's many translations (from the Russian, French, and German) include Alexandra Tolstoy's life of her father, Leo Tolstoy.

About the Artist

GABRIEL LISOWSKI was born in Jerusalem and grew up in Warsaw, Poland, and Vienna, Austria, where he now lives with his wife. He studied architecture in Vienna, but later switched to graphic design and illustration. Mr. Lisowski is the illustrator of THE WITCH OF FOURTH STREET AND OTHER STORIES by Myron Levoy.